TORTURED
SOULS

TORTURED SOULS

The Legend of Primordium

CLIVE BARKER

SUBTERRANEAN PRESS 2015

First Edition

ISBN
978-1-59606-636-6

Subterranean Press
PO Box 190106
Burton, MI 48519

subterraneanpress.com

BOOK ONE

The Secret
Face of
Genesis

I

HE IS A transformer of human flesh; a creator of monsters. If a Supplicant comes to him with sufficient need, sufficient hunger for change—knowing how painful that change will be—he will accommodate them. They become objects of perverse beauty beneath his hand; their bodies remade in fashions that they have no power to dictate.

Over the years, over the centuries, indeed, this extraordinary creature has gone by many names. But we will call him by the first name he was ever given: AGONISTES.

Where would a Supplicant find him? Usually in what he calls 'the burning places': deserts, for instance. But sometimes he can be found in 'the burning places' in our own inflamed cities: places where despair has seared away all belief in hope and love.

There he moves, silently, irreproachably, his presence barely more than a rumour. And there he waits for those who need him to come to find him.

When a Supplicant presents him or herself there is never coercion. There is never violence, at least until the Supplicant has signed over his or her flesh. Then yes, there may be some second thoughts, once the work begins. The truth is that on many occasions a Supplicant has begged to die rather than continue to be 'empowered' by Agonistes. It hurts too much, they tell him, as his scalpels and his torches work their terrible surgery upon him. But in all the time he has been wandering the world Agonistes has only ever granted the comfort of death to one Supplicant who changed his mind. That man was Judas Iscariot, who whined so much Agonistes hanged him from a tree. The rest he works on despite their complaints, sometimes for days and nights, coming back to his labours when a piece of flesh has healed and he can begin on the next part of the surgery.

There are some minor compensations for all this pain, which Agonistes will sometimes offer his Supplicants as he works. He will sing to them, for instance, and it is said that he knows every lullaby written, in every language of the world; songs of the cradle and the breast, to soothe the men and women he is remaking in the image of their terror.

And, if for some reason he feels particularly sympathetic to the Supplicant, Agonistes may even give his victim a piece of his own flesh to eat: just a sliver, cut with one of his finest scalpels, from the tender flesh of his upper thigh, or inner lip. According to legend, there is no food more comforting, more exquisite, than the flesh of Agonistes. The merest sliver of it upon the tongue of the Supplicant will make him or her forget all the horrors they are enduring, and deliver them to a place of paradisical calm.

Then once his client is soothed Agonistes continues his work, cutting, infibulating, searing, cauterizing, stretching, twisting, reconfiguring.

Sometimes he will bring a mirror to show his Supplicants what he has so far created. Sometimes he will announce that he wants the results to be a surprise; and so the Supplicant is left to imagine, through the haze of pain, what Agonistes is turning them into.

II

IT IS AN art, what Agonistes achieves.

He claims it is The First Art, this creation of new flesh, being the art God used to call life into being. Agonistes believes in God; prays to Him night and morning: thanking Him for making a world in which there is so much hopelessness and such a profound hunger for revenge that Supplicants will seek him out and beg him to reconfigure them in the image of their monstrous ideal.

And it appears that God apparently finds no offence in what Agonistes does, because for two and a half thousand years he has walked the planet, performing what he calls his holy art, and no harm has come to him. In fact he has prospered.

Some of the people who went under his knife, like Pontius Pilate, have a place in our culture's history. Many are anonymous. He has transformed potentates and gangsters, failed actors and architects; women who've been cheated by their husbands and come seeking a new form to greet their adulterer in their marriage beds;

school mistresses and perfumiers, dog-trainers and char-coal burners. The mighty and the insignificant, the noble and the peasant. As long as they are sincere Supplicants, and their prayers sound genuine, then Agonistes will be attentive to them.

Who is he, this Agonistes? This artist, this wanderer, this transformer of human flesh and bone?

In truth, nobody really knows. There is a heretical volume in the Vatican Library called 'A Treatise on the Madness of God', written by one Cardinal Gaillema in the mid-seventeenth century. In it, Gaillema argues that the account of the Creation of the world offered in the Book of Genesis is wrong in several particulars, one of which is relevant here: on the seventh day, the Cardinal argued, God did not rest. Instead, driven into a kind of ecstatic fugue state by the labours of His Creation, God continued to work. But the creations He summoned up in His exhausted state were not the wholesome beasts with which He had populated Eden. In one day and one night, wandering amongst the fresh glories of creation, He summoned up forms that defied all the beauty of his early work. Destroyers and demons, these were the antitheses of the wholesome forms that He had made in the first six days.

One of the creatures Jehovah created, the Cardinal claims, was Agonistes. That's why Agonistes can pray to His Father in Heaven, and expect to be listened to. He is—at least according to Cardinal Gaillema's account—one of God's own creations.

And there is no doubt that in his perverse way Agonistes serves a function. Over the years, over the centuries, he has been the answer to countless prayers for deliverance from powerlessness.

The words may change from prayer to prayer, but the meat of them is always the same:

"O Agonistes, dark deliverer, make me in the image of my enemies' nightmares. Let my flesh be the stuff from which you carve their terrors; let my skull be a bell which sounds their death-knell. Give me a song to sing, which will be the song of their despair, and let them wake and find me singing it at the bottom of their beds."

"Unmake me, unknit me, transform me."

"And if you cannot do that for me, Agonistes, then let me be excrement; let me be nothing; less than nothing."

"For I want to be the terror of my enemies, or I want oblivion."

"The choice, Lord, is yours."

BOOK TWO

The Assassin
Transformed

I

THE CITY OF Primordium was founded before any of the great cities of myth or history. Indeed, it is, according to many sources, the first city ever built. Before Troy, before Rome, before Jerusalem, there was Primordium.

Until recently it was ruled by a dynasty of Emperors, whose long tenure had steadily produced a capacity for cruelty that would have challenged the worst excesses of Rome's corrupted Caesars. The Emperor Perfetto XI, for instance, who controlled Primordium for sixteen years until the Great Insurrection, was a man familiar with every corruption of mind and spirit. He lived in excessive luxury, in a palace he believed impregnable, caring little or nothing for the two and three quarter million people who occupied Primordium.

In the end, that was his undoing.

But we'll come to that.

II

FIRST, LET ME tell you about Zarles Kreiger, who came from the lowest strata of the city. As a child, it was common for him to eat at the Vomitorium, where—as in ancient Rome—the rich food disgorged by the wealthy and overfed could be purchased for a small amount of money, and consumed a second time. It was Kreiger's good fortune that such a life of poverty did not kill him. By some physical paradox, experiences that would have reduced most men to shadows of their former selves, served to strengthen Zarles. By the time he was thirteen he was already larger than all his older brothers. And along with his physical prowess came something else: a curiosity about how the infinitely corrupt city in which he lived actually worked.

At the age of fourteen he became a runner for a gangster in the East City called Duraf Cascarellian, and quickly elevated himself in the criminal's employ, simply because he was willing to do anything requested of him. In return, Cascarellian treated Kreiger like a son; protecting him from capture by sending men out after Kreiger to clean up after one of his murders. Kreiger was a messy killer. Not for him the simple slit across the throat. He liked to use scythes, first disembowelling his victims then strangling them with their own entrails.

NOW SUCH BEHAVIOUR does not go unnoticed for long, even in a city as filled with excesses as Primordium. And Kreiger's reputation was increased considerably by the fact that the hits Cascarellian was having him make were often political. Judges, congressmen, journalists who were critical of the Emperor: these were often Kreiger's victims. Personally, he cared not at all about the affiliation of his victims. Blood was blood as far as Kreiger was concerned, and he took the same pleasure in it whether it poured from the flesh of a Republican or a Royalist.

Then he met a woman called Lucidique, and all that changed.

III

LUCIDIQUE WAS THE daughter of a Senator who had been lately complaining in open forum about the fact that the city was running into a state of decadence. The Perfetto Dynasty was using the people's taxes to fund its own pleasures, the Senator argued: it had to stop.

The order quickly came down from the Emperor: rid me of this Senator. Cascarellian, not giving a damn about the philosophical issues, but happy to oblige his Emperor, sent Kreiger out to kill the political troublemaker.

Kreiger went to the Senator's estate, caught him in the garden amongst his roses, gutted him and carried him inside. He was in the act of arranging the Senator's body on the dinner table, when Lucidique entered. She was naked, having just come from bathing. But she was also prepared for the intruder. She carried two knives.

She circled Kreiger, as he stood amongst the blood and the innards of her father.

"If you move I'll kill you," she said.

"With two table knives?" Kreiger said, slicing the air with his scythes. "Go back to your bath and forget I was here."

"This was my father you just murdered!"

"Yes. I see the resemblance."

"I would have thought a man like you would have thought twice about taking a knife to my father's throat. He wanted to overthrow the Empire so that you and your like would not be exploited."

"Me and my like? You don't know anything about me."

"I can guess," Lucidique said. "You were born in filth, and you've lived in filth so long you don't even see what's going on right in front of you."

Kreiger's expression changed. "So perhaps you do know a little," he said, his voice uneasy. The woman's confidence unnerved him. "I will leave you to mourn your father," he said, retreating from the table.

"Wait!" the woman said. "Not so quickly."

"What do you mean: wait? I could kill you in a heartbeat if I wanted to."

"But you don't want to, or you would have done it."

"What's your name?"

"Lucidique."

"So then, what do you want from me?"

"I want you to come with me, into the filthiest streets of Primordium."

"Believe me, I've seen them."

"Then you show me."

IV

IT WAS THE strangest walk a man and a woman ever took together. Though Kreiger had washed the Senator's

24

blood from his face, hands, and arms he still stank of murder. And here he was, walking beside the daughter of the man he'd just murdered, wrapped in dark linen.

Together, they saw the worst of Primordium: the disease, the violence, and the grinding, unrelieved poverty. And every now and then Lucidique would point to the walls and the towers of the Emperor's Winter Palace, any one room of which contained sufficient wealth to clear the slums of the city, and feed every starving child.

And for the first time in many, many years Kreiger felt some measure of real emotion, remembering circumstances of his own upbringing, left to sit in the open sewers of Primordium's streets while his mother sold her drug-riddled body to one of the Emperor's guards. There was anger in him as he walked. And it steadily grew.

"What do you want me to do?" he said, frustrated by what he felt, and his own helplessness. "I could never get to the Emperor."

"Don't be so sure."

"What do you mean?"

"You're right, the Dynasty is untouchable as long as you're just a man; a scabby little assassin hired to kill overweight Senators. But suppose you could be more than that? Then you could bring the Dynasty down."

"How?"

Lucidique gave Kreiger a sideways glance. "It's nothing I can show you here. Besides, I have a father to bury. If you want to know more, then meet me tomorrow night outside the Western Gates. Come alone."

"If this is some kind of trap..." Kreiger said, "...some way to revenge your father...then before they take me I'll cut out your eyes."

Lucidique smiled. "You make such pretty love-talk," she said.

"I mean it."

"I know. And I wouldn't be so stupid as to conspire against you. Quite the reverse. I believe we were meant to know one another. I was meant to walk in on your killing my father, and you were meant to hold your hand off and not kill me. There's some connection between us. You feel it, don't you?"

Kreiger looked at the dirty street between them. The night had been filled with feelings he had not anticipated experiencing. And now here was another; admitting to the strange intimacy he felt for the daughter of the man he'd murdered.

"Yes," he said. "I feel it." Then, after a long silence: "What time tomorrow night?"

"Sometime after one," Lucidique told him. "I'll be there."

V

THE FOLLOWING DAY the streets of Primordium were alive with gossip and speculation: the death of the Senator had started all kinds of rumours. Was this murder the first indication that the Emperor would put up with no more moves towards democracy in the city? Believing this to be the case many members of the Senate left Primordium hurriedly, in case, they were next on the Emperor's hit list. There was a general sense of unrest, everywhere.

And in Kreiger, a profound sense of anticipation.

He had barely slept, thinking of what had happened the night before. No, not just the night before. Thinking about his life: where it had led him so far, and where— if Lucidique's promise were a true one—it would go after this.

Every now and then he'd glance towards the walls of the palace (which had twice as many guards patrolling them today as yesterday) and wonder to himself what she had meant about finding a way for one man to bring down a Dynasty?

VI

AT ONE O'CLOCK in the morning, a mile outside the West Gate of Primordium, he sat on a stone and he waited. At nine minutes past one, a pair of horses approached (not from the city, from which direction Kreiger had expected her to come, but from the Desert, which lay, vast and largely uncharted, out to the West and South-West of the city).

They drew nearer, and dismounted.

"Kreiger…"

"Yes?"

"I want you to meet Agonistes."

Kreiger had heard rumours about this man Agonistes. It was the kind of story that was exchanged between assassins, more of a legend than a reality.

But here he was. As real as the woman who'd brought him.

"I hear you want to make Primordium a Republic," Agonistes said. "Single-handed."

"She persuaded me it was possible," Kreiger replied. "But...I don't believe it is."

"You should have more faith, Kreiger. I can make you the terror of Emperors, if you want it badly enough. It's up to you. Make up your mind quickly, for I have better business elsewhere tonight if you don't require my services. I can hear a hundred prayers pouring out of Primordium at this very moment; people wanting me to give them the power to change their world."

Lucidique put her hand up to Kreiger's face. "Now the moment's here, I see you don't want it," she said. "You're afraid."

"I'm not afraid!" Kreiger said. He thought of his mother, dead of the pox, of his brothers killed in the street as children by noblemen passing on horses, of his sister, in the asylum, never to be sane again.

"Take me," he said.

"You're sure?" Agonistes asked him. "Remember, there's no way back."

"I don't want to go back. Take me. Change me."

He glanced at Lucidique. She was smiling.

"Take the horses," Agonistes told her. "We won't need them."

So together, Kreiger and Agonistes turned round and headed into the desert.

VII

THE NEXT DAY Lucidique buried her father. The rumours quietened down a little in the city, but there was still an undercurrent, subtle but pervasive: Primordium was in a very volatile state; like an explosive, which might be set off with a jolt.

Eight nights after Agonistes had taken Kreiger out into the desert, Lucidique—whose father's house lay close to the palace—woke to the sounds of screams.

She got up, and went to the window. There were lights burning in all the palace windows. The gates were flung wide. Guards were running around in confusion.

She dressed, anonymously, and went down into the streets. The din had woken the city; and though the Emperor's guards were riding back and forth, attempting to enforce an on-the-spot curfew, nobody was attending to them.

Lucidique went into the palace. The screams had died down now, to be replaced by half-whispered prayers.

But it didn't take her very long to discover what the creature who had once been Zarles Kreiger had wrought. There was death on every side. And his slaughter had been indiscriminate: men and women, yes; but also their children, their babies; their unborn babies.

The Perfetto Empire ceased to rule Primordium that night. There were none left alive to do so. Kreiger had killed them all.

As Lucidique stood in the Great Hall of the Palace, in a pool of blood that reached to the walls, she caught a reflection. She looked up.

There he was. Kreiger, remade. THE SCYTHE-MEISTER. There was almost nothing left of the man she'd known: Agonistes' handiwork had transformed the humble assassin into something that would haunt the nightmares, and the streets, of Primordium, for many years to come.

He approached her. She wondered if this was her last moment; if he intended to kill her as efficiently as he'd dispatched all the rest. But no. He simply leaned down and whispered in her ear:

"...you cannot imagine..."

Then he left the carnage behind him, and wandered out into the night, pausing only to wash his blades in one of the many fountains in the courtyards.

BOOK THREE

The
Avenger

I

ZARLES KREIGER WAS human once. An assassin work-ing for the gangster Duraf Cascarellian, Kreiger was a man who would do anything for a price. But there are some tasks that have an unforeseen price, and this proved to be one of them. Caught red-handed by the Senator's daughter, the exquisite Lucidique, Kreiger was persuaded that he in his turn had been a victim. The rulers of the city in which they all lived—the vast, degenerate city-state of Primordium—were the truly guilty souls; and until the dynasty was brought down life would continue to be a bloody confusion in which men like Kreiger acted like rabid animals and women like Lucidique lost their loved ones.

It had to stop. And Lucidique knew how. She per-suaded Kreiger to put himself into the hands of an ancient entity called Agonistes, who would traumatically recon-figure him.

He did as Lucidique suggested, and after eight days and nights out in the desert, he returned to Primordium as The Scythe-Meister: a powerful engine of destruction, who in a matter of hours brought the Perfetto Dynasty to a close.

Before disappearing into the desert, he had three words for Lucidique, three teasing words:

"...you cannot imagine..."

II

THEY CALLED THAT night—the night the Emperor and his family were murdered—the Great Insurrection. In its wake, a host of minor insurrections took place, as old enmities erupted. Powerful figures who'd used the decadent reign of the Emperor Perfetto as a cover for their corruptions—judges, bishops, members of the clergy, guild and union leaders—found themselves unprotected, and face to face with the people they'd exploited.

Even those amongst the criminal classes who had private armies to protect them against this very eventuality were fearful now.

Take, for example, Duraf Cascarellian. He wasn't by any means a stupid man. The fact that his assassin, Zarles Kreiger, had disappeared the night of the Insurrection made him highly suspicious that Kreiger's fate was tied in with the almost supernatural fall of the Emperor. Indeed one of Cascarellian's spies, who had been a guard at the palace the night of the slaughter, had seen the creature everyone called The Scythe-Meister washing his weapons in one of the Palace's many fountains. The informant had escaped the massacre without harm coming to him, and reported that unlikely as it seemed, the semi-mythical figure of The Scythe-Meister bore a subtle but undeniable resemblance to Zarles Kreiger.

Was it possible, Cascarellian wondered, that the missing assassin and The Scythe-Meister were somehow the same person? Had some incomprehensible sea-change been worked upon Kreiger, turning him into this unstoppable avenger? And if so, what part did Lucidique—who had been seen in a brief exchange with The Scythe-Meister—play in the proc

III

CASCARELLIAN DID NOT sleep well any longer. He had nightmares in which The Scythe-Meister broke down his doors, as it had broken down the doors of the Emperor's Palace, killing his lieutenants, as it had slaughtered the palace guards, and finally come to the foot of his bed—as the killer had come to the Emperor's bed, pulling him limb from limb.

He decided the best way to protect himself from this unknowable force was through Lucidique. He sent three of his sons out to take the Senator's daughter captive, ordering them to do as little as possible to arouse her wrath. In his heart (though he would never have admitted this to anyone, not even his priest) he was a little afraid of Lucidique. She needed to be treated with more respect than he was used to proffering women.

Unfortunately, his offspring weren't as smart as he was. Though they'd been told to respect their captive, they took the first opportunity to test the limits of their father's patience. Lucidique was taunted, abused, humiliated. No doubt worse would have come her way had Old Man Cascarellian not returned from his day of business early, interrupting his sons' taunting of the woman.

Lucidique instantly demanded to know why she was being held. If Cascarellian intended to kill her, why the hell didn't he get on with it? She was sick and tired, she told him. Of him, of his sons, of life itself. She'd seen too much blood.

"You were at the Palace, weren't you? The Night of the Great Insurrection?"

"Yes. I was there."

"You have something to do with this creature: this Scythe-Meister?"

"My business, Cascarellian."

"I could give you to my sons for half an hour. They'd have it out of you!"

"Your sons don't intimidate me. And neither do you."

"I don't wish to make you uncomfortable. You're here under my protection; that's all. Do you know what it's like out there on our streets? Pandemonium! The city is coming apart at the seams!"

"Do you think holding me here is going to protect you from what's coming your way?" Lucidique said.

A look of superstitious fear crossed Cascarellian's face. "What's coming my way?" he said. "You know something about the future?"

"No," Lucidique said wearily. "I'm not a prophet. I don't know what's going to happen to you and frankly I don't care. If the world ends tomorrow, I don't think you'll be judged very kindly, but—" she shrugged, "—why should I care? I won't be there to see you suffer in Hell."

Cascarellian had grown pale and clammy while Lucidique spoke. She only half-knew what she was doing to him, but she took a certain pleasure in it. This was the man who'd orphaned her; why not enjoy his superstitious fear?

"You think I'm a stupid man?" he said.

"To be afraid the way you're afraid now? Yes. I think that's pitiful."

"I don't want your contempt," Cascarellian said, with a strange sincerity. "I have enough enemies."

"Then don't make one of me," Lucidique said. "Let me go. Let me see the sky!"

"I'll take you out, if that's what you want."

"You will?"

"Yes. We'll go wherever you like."

"I want to go out into the desert. Away from the city."

"Really? Why?"

"I told you. I want to see the sky…"

IV

THE NEXT DAY, a convoy of three cars wound through the chaotic streets of Primordium and headed for the West Gate. In the first car, two of Cascarellian's best men—loyal bodyguards who'd seen him through many attempts upon his life. In the back car, the three brothers, wondering aloud (as they increasingly did these days) if a kind of lunacy had overtaken their father. Why was he indulging this woman Lucidique in her whims? Didn't he understand that she had every reason to hate him, to plot against him?

In the middle car, chauffeured by Marius, Cascarellian's driver for three decades, sat the Don himself, accompanied by Lucidique.

"Satisfied?" he said to her, once they were outside the gates, and in sight of the open sky.

"A little further, please…" she said.

"Don't think you can fool me, woman. You may be cleverer than most of your sex, but you won't escape me, if that's your thought!"

They drove on in silence for a distance.

"I think we've come far enough. And you've seen enough of the sky for one day!"

"Can't I just get out and walk?"

"Walking now, is it?"

"Please. There's no harm in that surely? Look…open ground in every direction."

Cascarellian considered this for a moment. Then he called the convoy to a halt.

A dust storm was on the horizon, slowly approaching the road.

"You'd better be quick!" the Don told her.

Lucidique watched the approaching wall of sand, then glanced round at the men who were getting out of the cars; particularly the brothers. They smiled slyly as they eyed her. One of them flicked his tongue between his lips, the obscene inference plain.

It was the last straw. Lucidique turned her back on him—on them all—and began to walk towards the sandstorm.

A chorus of warnings instantly erupted behind her. "Don't take another step!" one of the brothers said, "or I'll shoot you!"

She turned to him, her arms opened wide. "So shoot!" she said.

Then she turned again and strode on.

"Come back here, woman!" the Don yelled. "There's nothing out there but sand."

The wind from the storm was whipping up Lucidique's hair now. It was like a dark halo around her head.

"Do you hear me?" the Don called after her.

Lucidique looked over her shoulder.

"Come walk with me," she said to him.

The old man drew hard on his cigar, and then went after the woman.

His sons set up a chorus of complaint: what was he doing? Was he out of his mind?

He ignored them. He simply followed in Lucidique's footsteps across the sand.

She glanced over her shoulder at the old man, who wore a curious expression. In some strange way he was happy at that moment; happier than he'd been in many years, with the wind hot against his face, and the beautiful woman calling to him to come with her—

Seeing that he was obeying her, she returned her gaze to the sandstorm, which was now no more than a hundred yards off. There was something moving at its heart. She was not surprised. Though she hadn't planned the reunion that lay ahead she had nevertheless known in her heart that it was coming. Her life since she'd stepped into her father's death-chamber, and seen Kreiger at work, had been like a strange dream, which she was somehow shaping without conscious effort.

She stopped walking. Cascarellian had caught up with her and seized her arm. He had a knife in the other hand. He pressed it to her breast.

"So that's where he is!" said Cascarellian, staring at the dark giant in the heart of the storm. "Your Scythe-Meister."

As he spoke, the sandstorm picked up a sudden spurt of speed and came at them—

"Don't come any closer!" the Don warned the creature in the storm. "I'll kill her."

He pressed the knife into Lucidique's skin, just enough to draw blood.

"Tell him to keep his distance," he warned.

"It isn't Kreiger. It's a man called Agonistes. He has God's fingerprints upon him."

The heresy of this made Cascarellian's devoted stomach turn. "Don't talk that way!" he said, and with a sudden spurt of righteousness he drove the knife into her heart. She reached out, and touched the wound, then with her finger bloody, grazed his forehead. A death mark.

Cascarellian let the body drop to the ground and ordered a quick retreat to the cars before the storm reached them. This grim business wasn't finished, just because she was dead. He knew that. It was just beginning.

HE TURNED THE house into a fortress. He had the windows sealed, and blessed with holy water. He bricked up the chimneys. He had guards and dogs patrolling the place night and day.

After a week he began to believe that perhaps his faith and his gifts of money to the diocese, buying congregations praying for his safety, were having some effect.

He started to relax.

Then, on the afternoon of the eighth day, a wind came out of the West: a sandy wind. It hissed at the sealed doors and the windows. It whined beneath the floorboards. The old man took two tranquilizers and a glass of wine, and went to sit in his bath.

A pleasant torpor overcame him as he sat in the warm water. His eyes fluttered closed.

And then her voice. Somehow she'd got in. She'd survived the knife to her heart and she'd got in.

"Look at you," she said. "Naked as a baby."

He grabbed his towel to cover himself, but as he did so she stepped out of the shadows and showed herself to him, in all her terrible glory. She was not the Lucidique he'd known; not remotely. Her whole body was transformed. She'd become a living weapon.

"Oh Jesus help me..." he murmured.

She reached forward and she castrated him with one sweep of her scythe. He clamped his bloody hands to his empty groin and stumbled out to the landing, calling for help. But the house was silent from roof to cellar. He called his sons' names, one by one. None came. Only his old dog Malleus answered his call, and when he trotted through from the kitchen he left red paw-marks on the white carpet. He was eating something human.

"All dead," Lucidique said.

Then, very gently, she took hold of the back of Cascarellian's neck, the way a mother-cat catches hold of an errant kitten, and lifted him up, effortlessly. The blood from his vacant groin slapped against the carpet.

She put her blade to his chest and cut out his heart. Then she let his body tumble back down the stairs.

Later, when the wind had dropped, and she could see the stars clearly, she went out into the street, leaving the door to the Cascarellian mansion wide open so that the atrocity there should be soon discovered. Then she headed out, through a variety of back streets and alleys, to the West Gate, and thence into the waiting desert.

BOOK FOUR

The Surgeon
of the
Sacred Heart

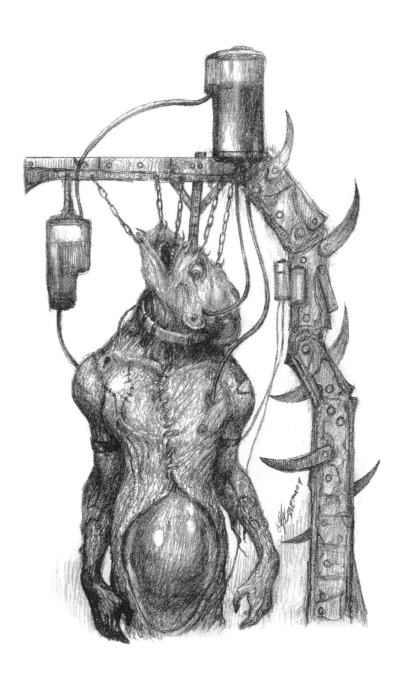

and upon girls of six or seven in the case of Montefalco). Second, a startling capacity for superstition.

It went undiscussed, but they each knew the other was touched by a profound fear of the uncanny. And there was no city presently more inundated in unholy matters than Primordium. Rumour was rife here; and its subject was seldom rational. The stories that were passed around the soldiers' campfires (and sooner or later reached the Generals' ears) were of unnatural horrors: things that defied reason. Tales of monsters that had been bred from the loins of The Scythe-Meister; of the vengeful ghosts of children; of succubi, their sexual attributes discussed in clammy, but arousing detail.

ONE NIGHT, AFTER some very heavy drinking, the three men vented their fears.

"It is my belief," Urbano said, "that this damned city is haunted."

The other two men nodded grimly.

"What do you suggest we do about it?" Bogoto asked.

It was Montefalco who replied. "Well, for a start…if I had my druthers I'd burn the illegal immigrant quarter to the ground. It's they who engage in most of these unholy goings-on."

"But the work-force…" Bogoto said. "Who'd empty our shit cans? Who'd bury the lepers?"

Montefalco had to concede the point. "At least we could target any element we suspect of intercourse with demonic forces."

"Good. Good," said Urbano. "Vigilance."

"And punishment," Montefalco went on. "Swift, draconian measures—"

"Public executions."

"Yes!"

"Burnings?"

"No, too theatrical. Shootings are clean and fast. And they don't smell."

"That bothers you?" said Bogoto.

Montefalco shuddered. "I loathe the smell of burning bodies," he said.

II

WHILE THE GENERALS debated the relative merits of this kind of execution or that, Lucidique was sleeping— or attempting to sleep—in the house which her father had built many years ago for her mother. Her slumbers were uneasy. So many memories. So many regrets.

Often in earlier, simpler times, when sleep eluded her, she would go out walking. Now, of course, she could not go by day. The transformation of her body that had been wrought by Agonistes had resulted in a physique which was strong, supple and powerful, but which terrified many who laid eyes on her. When she did go out—even in the blackest night—she did her best to keep to the quiet back-alleys of Primordium where she would not be seen.

TONIGHT, HAVING GIVEN up on sleep, she went wandering in these alleys, and became aware that she was being followed.

After a little distance she sensed the rhythm of the step, and realized that she knew who her pursuer was. It was Zarles Kreiger, the assassin turned Scythe-Meister.

She stopped, and turned.

The Scythe-Meister was standing a little distance from her. His flesh had the same sickly luminescence that hers did; a bacterial brightness that was part of Agonistes' handiwork. The rawer the wounds (and there were parts of both their transformed bodies that were designed to never heal) the brighter the luminescence with which they burned.

"I thought you'd left the city," she said to him.

"I did. For a while. I went out into the desert. Meditated on my changed state."

"And did you learn anything from your meditations?"

Kreiger shook his head.

"So you came back?"

"So I came back."

III

A FEW DAYS after the three Generals had exchanged their fears about the presence of unsacred powers in Primordium, Montefalco brought them together again for a midnight journey.

"Where are we going?"

"There's a man called Doctor Talisac who has been conducting experiments on my behalf for several years now."

"What kind of experiments?" Urbano wanted to know.

"I hoped he would perfect me a soldier. Make a fighting machine that was not susceptible to fear."

"Has he succeeded?"

"No. Not so far. Nor do I have great hope for him now. He's addicted to many of his own medications, and...well, you'll see for yourself. But there was one failure of his which might be useful to us now."

"A useful failure?" Bogoto said, somewhat amused by the paradox.

"We need a creature that will drive the unholy elements out of Primordium. I believe he has such a creature."

"Ah..." said Urbano.

"So will you see this creature with me?"

"Where is he?"

"I have him hidden away in what used to be the Hospice of the Sacred Heart, on Dreyfus Hill."

"I thought the place was empty."

"That's the impression I intended to give the world. If anybody ventures in there I have them killed and thrown in the canal."

"Is that what happened to the nuns?"

Montefalco smiled. "Nothing so humane, I'm afraid," he said. "Soldiers can be brutish if left to their own devices."

The subject was left there, and the three headed up towards Dreyfus Hill.

IV

ZARLES KREIGER STRETCHED out naked on Lucidique's bed. She looked at him admiringly: at the plethora of scars; at the intricate way the machinations of his flesh had been bound to Agonistes' own creations. Silver bonded with bone and nerve; gold and bronze the same.

She climbed on top of him. Arcs of electricity leapt between them: nipple to nipple, eye to eye.

What a time this was! she thought. Here she was mating with the man who had taken her father's life. In a sense there was something even more taboo about their intimacy. They were both the offspring of the same father. Both Agonistes' children.

"I wonder if he'd approve?" Lucidique said.

"You mean Agonistes?"

"Yes."

Kreiger didn't speak. It was Lucidique who realized what her lover's reference to Agonistes implied.

"You saw him in the desert?"

"Yes."

"And he sent you back here?"

"Yes."

"To find me?"

"To be with you. He said you were the only thing that would make me happy."

V

THE HOSPICE OF the Sacred Heart was an enormous edifice, its upper floors in darkness. But the Generals didn't have to wait long for a guide. After a few minutes a female dwarf—who introduced herself as Camille—came with candles. She escorted the uniformed trio through the echoing cloisters (which were heaped with huge mounds of dirt) and down two flights of steep stairs into Doctor Talisac's laboratory.

His workspace had been dug out of the earth so as to accommodate the scale of the Doctor's experimentation and still preserve the secrecy of his location. In place of tile there was hard-trodden earth beneath the Generals' boots, and the walls were beaten dirt. The place stank of cold earth: which served to complete the scene. For if the stench was that of the grave, so were many of the sights before them. The dead were Talisac's raw materials, and they lay everywhere around, in various states of amputation. He was an uneconomic consumer. In many cases the corpses were lacking only a limb, or a portion of a limb; an eye, in one case, lips in another.

"So where is he?" Urbano demanded to know.

Camille pointed the way over a carpet of corpses to a dank corner of the immense chamber, where Talisac awaited them.

He looked, to the Generals' astonished eyes, like one of his own victims; a terrible, implausible experiment in the extremes to which a human carcass might be put.

He hung by his mouth from a device whose purpose was beyond the Generals' comprehension, his mouth hooked up, as though he were a fish. In his perversity, or his genius, or both, he had created some kind of external womb for himself. A semi-translucent bag hung from the lower portion of his abdomen, down between his spidery legs. There was life inside.

"A Mongroid," Camille whispered.

Montefalco took his eyes off the foul sight of the womb and its twitching contents, and addressed its owner.

"Talisac?" he said. "We need something from you."

Talisac turned his fluttering eyes in Montefalco's direction. When he spoke, the maimed form of his mouth meant that what he said was virtually incomprehensible. It took Camille to translate it.

"He says: 'What? What do you need?'"

"We need a fiend to put fear into the heart of the Devil himself," Montefalco said. "A beast amongst beasts. Something to scour the city of its monsters by being still more monstrous."

Talisac made a strange sound—which might have been laughter; shaking as he hung from his hooks. The creature in his womb responded to its parent's movement by spasming.

"How the hell did he come by that thing?" Bogoto murmured to Urbano behind his hand.

"Don't whisper," Camille snapped. "He hates it."

"He was wondering how Talisac got himself pregnant?" Urbano said.

This time Talisac pressed his lips into service, in order that he answer for himself. The reply was a single word:

"Science," he said.

"Really?" Urbano said, sufficiently reassured to step over some of the mutilated bodies to examine Talisac more closely. "Well I'm pleased to hear that. I would have been distressed if there's been some sexual impropriety here."

Again, Talisac laughed, though none of the Generals were in the mood to see the humour of the situation. His laughter spent, he spoke again. This time Camille's services as a translator were required.

"He has a golem he thinks would suit your purposes very well," the dwarf said. "He only asks one thing in return…"

"And what's that?" Montefalco said.

"That you shouldn't attempt to hurt any of his children."

"Meaning that?" Montefalco said, nodding towards the twitching womb.

"Es," said Talisac. "Is my ur chile."

"What did he say?" Urbano said to Camille.

"He said it was his child," Camille replied.

Montefalco shrugged.

"No harm will come of this Mongroid, if we are given a fiend of our own," Montefalco said. "I will personally guarantee that."

"Good," said Camille. Then, without Talisac speaking again, she added: "He would prefer if you did not come here again together. Only General Montefalco."

"You'll get no argument from me on that account," Bogoto said, waving the horror away as he retreated. "If he gives us our monster, then he can give birth to a thousand little brats as far as I'm concerned. Just keep them the hell away from me."

VI

LUCIDIQUE LAY ON the blood- and sweat-stained bed beside her lover, and watched the moon through the window.

"This can't last for long, you know. This thing between us."

CLIVE BARKER

"Why not?"

"For two such as us to find some happiness together?" she said. "It's against nature. You killed my father. I should hate you."

"And you put me through hell at Agonistes' hands. I should hate you."

"What a pair we make."

"Maybe we should go back out into the desert," Kreiger said. "We'd be safer there."

Lucidique laughed. "Listen to you. Safer! Isn't the world supposed to be afraid of us? Not the other way round."

"I just want to hold on to this...hope that I feel."

Lucidique reached across the bed and ran her blade along Kreiger's arm. "We can't leave Primordium," she said.

"Why not? It's going up in flames, sooner or later. Let it burn."

"But love, we started the fire, you and me. We should stay and watch it to the end."

Kreiger nodded. "If that's what you want."

"It's the way things have to end."

"End? Why do you say that?"

"Hush, love. It'll be better this way, you'll see." She leaned over and kissed him. "Do it for me."

"That's as good a reason as any I ever heard," Kreiger said.

"So you'll stay?"

"I'll stay."

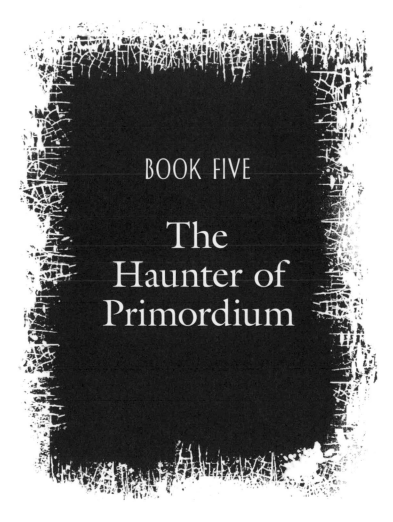

BOOK FIVE

The
Haunter of
Primordium

I

HAVING MADE THE arrangement with Talisac to provide them with a creature, the three Generals— Bogoto, Urbano and Montefalco—returned to Military Headquarters and waited. Bogoto was the most anxious of the three. He'd seen his share of battle scenes; bodies blown to pieces, the stink of burning hair and bone in the air: but the grotesqueries of Talisac's laboratory had left him sickened and nervous.

He decided to do what he often did when his life became difficult: he drove across the city in the night to seek the comfort of a woman called Greta Sabatier, a reader of fortunes. Though he would have been appalled if he'd thought any of his fellow Generals knew it, Sabatier's advice had been behind much of what Bogoto had done over the years: who he'd favoured amongst his subordinates, and who he'd demoted; even, on occasion, how he'd run some of his military campaigns. And as events in Primordium had steadily become more crazed, Bogoto had come to rely more and more upon Sabatier's wisdom. Her cards, he had come to believe, carried vital clues to his fate. In a world where madness was constantly in the air, and nothing and no one could be trusted, it made a paradoxical sense to seek illumination from a woman who read the future from a pack of dirty cards.

"You've seen somebody powerful," Greta told him that night, tapping one of the cards she'd just turned over. "I can't tell if it's a man…or a woman."

Bogoto pictured Talisac, hanging up from his hooks, with that vile womb of his hanging down between his legs.

Sabatier was studying his face.

"You know this person I'm talking about?"

Bogoto nodded.

"Well then you don't need any warning from me. He, or she—which is it?"

"It's a man."

"Well he has friends…allies…it's hard to be sure exactly who or what they are…the cards are very ambiguous. But there's harm from this source, whatever it is."

"Harm to me?"

"Harm to the world."

"Huh."

"That matters less to you, yes?"

"Of course. Do you think I should consider leaving the city?"

"Well…you're a military man. It's not the first time I've seen death in your cards, General."

This was the first time Greta had ever made mention of the General's profession. Whether she knew it from the cards or from the broadsheets in which he was regularly eulogized was anybody's guess.

"But I don't think I ever saw it so near to you," she went on, looking at the cards.

"I see."

"So yes, I think you should consider leaving. At least until this unsettled period is over astronomically."

"So it's not just the cards, it's the stars too?"

"They're all reflections of one another: cards, stars, palms. It's the same story wherever you look."

She sorted through the cards as she spoke, and now dropped one down on the table in front of General Bogoto. It was called The Tower, and it represented—in a simplified, even crude, form—a tower struck by lightning. Its upper half was erupting, raining down rubble, and bodies; the lower half was cracked and ready to topple.

"This is Primordium?" Bogoto said.

"It's the city's future," Greta replied, nodding. "Or at least one of them."

"So will you be leaving too?" Bogoto said, thinking to catch the woman out. Greta was as old as the antiquated table she read her cards upon and her legs were a good deal less reliable. She'd never leave Primordium; or so he thought.

"Yes, I'm leaving. This will be the last time you see me, General, unless you should come to Calyx."

"You're moving to Calyx?"

"Tomorrow. Before things get any worse."

II

THE HOUSE ON Diamanda Street, which had once belonged to the murdered Senator, had gathered itself quite a reputation of late.

There were lovers there, it was rumoured; several of them. Night and day, passers-by heard the sound of love-making: the sighs, the sobs, the irresistible demands.

The houses nearby were all virtually deserted, their owners having fled Primordium for safer cities; or better still, for the country. Life on a pig-farm might be boring, but at least it had a chance of being long. Nevertheless people came to Diamanda Street of late, simply to hear the noise of pleasure out of the lamp-lit home. No, not just to hear. There was a feeling about the place, which got under people's skin. The energy seeping out from open windows was enough to make the fireflies assemble in their many tens of thousands each dusk and describe elaborate arabesques in their pursuit of one another, the air so thick with their passion, and their light so insistent, that the house was festooned with their flight paths, which lingered long after the deed was done and the insects lay exhausted and extinguished in the long grass.

Sometimes the human voyeurs, who lingered in the shadows of the nearby houses, hoping to catch a glimpse of the lovers, were granted what they were here to see. As the strange force of the lover's din suggested, they were not natural creatures, not by any means. They seemed to be hybrids; one third human, one third metallic, one third the no-man's land between flesh and devices made to strip it and slash it and scour it. They bled as they rose from their nuptial sheets; but smiled, kissing one another's wounds as though they were inconsequential, as though these flaps and sores and gougings were proof of devotion.

Word got round, quickly enough. It didn't take long for General Montefalco to hear about the house on

Diamanda Street, and the reputation it had got for itself. He went to the location, late one night. Things were in full swing: the air filled with weaving lights, the houses moaning and shaking. Then shrieks of terrible joy out of the fire-lit interior, and shadows on the blinds, moving from room to room as the momentum of the lovers' passion carried them around the house.

Montefalco had never seen, heard, or felt anything like it before. A wave of something like superstition passed through his body, weakening his bowels and making his hair, which was a quarter inch from widow's peak to nape, stand on end.

He started to retreat from the house, clammy-palmed. As he did so he heard a voice behind him. He turned. It was Urbano. He looked like a man who had just discovered some truly terrible thing about himself, or God, or both.

"These we kill," Montefalco said, very calmly.

General Urbano began to nod, but the motion was too much for his sickened system. He puked a yellowish puke, which spattered his immaculately polished boots. He took out a handkerchief and wiped his mouth; then he said:

"Yes."

"Yes?"

"Yes. These we kill."

Later that night, Montefalco went back to see Talisac. He went alone, which turned out to be a wise move. Neither Urbano nor Bogoto had the guts for what awaited him there.

The place had deteriorated considerably in the forty-eight hours since he'd last stepped over the threshold;

the bodies were still everywhere, but they were in a new condition. It looked as though all the moisture, all the energy, had been sucked out of them, leaving them withered. The eyes had gone from the sockets and the lips had been drawn back from the teeth, giving them all the look of blind, squealing monkeys.

The flesh on their torsos had withered to bones, as had the meat on their arms and legs. The skin itself was now like a thin layer of dried tissue, covering the structure of the bone. When the dwarf Camille appeared to greet Montefalco, and kicked a couple of the corpses aside, they rolled away from her kick like so many paper mannequins.

"Is it done?" Montefalco asked her.

"Oh yes, it's done," Camille said with a twinkling smile, "and I think you're going to be very pleased."

A voice emerged from the shadows, speaking words Montefalco could not comprehend.

"He's asking me to unveil it," Camille said.

The General scanned the dirt-walled room, looking for what 'it' might be; and there at the end of the chamber he saw a monumental form, covered with a threadbare tapestry obviously brought down from the floor above.

"That?" he said, not waiting for confirmation before approaching it. As he strode through the bodies, they cracked beneath his heels, erupting into dust and fragments. Soon the room was filled with spiralling bits of pale human stuff.

Montefalco grabbed hold of the tapestry. As he did so, Camille named the thing—

"Venal Anatomica."

The General pulled the tapestry off and revealed it.

As might have been guessed from its scale beneath the carpet, it was of heroic size, nine feet tall or more. It had death's face, and was equipped with a variety of medieval murder weapons. There were nails crudely hammered into its shoulder and leg. Blood had coagulated around the nails, but when Anatomica began to move (as now it did) fresh blood bubbled up from the wounds and ran down his body.

"Does it know me?" the General asked.

"Yes," said Camille, "it is ready to obey your instructions." Talisac spoke, and Camille translated. "He says he has no loyalty to its Creator, only to you, General Montefalco."

"That's good to hear."

Montefalco beckoned to it.

"Come on then."

The creature made a hesitant step. Then another.

"Can I come with you?" Camille said.

Montefalco looked down at her nakedness. "Only if you cover yourself up," he said.

She smiled, and then went away to fetch herself a flea-bitten fur coat.

They went out into the night together: the three of them. The General, the Dwarf and Venal Anatomica.

Daybreak wasn't far off. Neither was the end of certain things. Though Greta Sabatier had been killed by the bandits on the road to Calyx—a fate she had not foreseen—she had been right about that much. An age was coming to an end: and it was the Age of Lovers.

BOOK SIX

The Second
Coming

I

IN HIS BUNKER of dirt and corpses Talisac waited alone, while his body—which was a thing without precedent—twitched and jumped and spasmed.

There was a child inside of him; the Mongroid, the infant of the Second Coming. Or so he'd come to believe, after the years he'd spent experimenting upon others, and himself. It wasn't until he had created an homunculus that would be to all intents and purposes his child, its flesh made up of the same DNA as his, that he had come to believe there was something holy in the imminent arrival. It was another Virgin Birth.

In only a matter of hours now, the child would be in his arms.

He would have no one to share the triumph of what he'd achieved, but so be it. He'd been alone all his life, even in the company of his fellow human beings. Alone with his ambition, alone with his failures, alone with the strange dreams that came to find him in the middle of the night; dreams of his child, speaking to him, telling him that the world was going to end, but that it wouldn't matter, because they'd be together, Man and Child, to the End of Time.

He could feel the child struggling to get out now. He could hear its tiny, high-pitched voice as it worked to free itself.

The pain was excruciating; a vicious hallucinogen. He sobbed and he screamed; the Convent had never heard such cursings as it heard now.

But finally the womb tore as the Holy Child scrabbled with his little hands, his little nails, and in a gush of blood-tinged fluids the Mongroid was disgorged onto the ground amongst the corpses.

II

"KREIGER?"

Lucidique went to the window and called down into the garden around her father's house. Zarles Kreiger, The Scythe-Meister, who had lately become Lucidique's lover, had gone out into the garden to bring her some perfumed flowers. The bedroom stank of the pungent oil that their violently transfigured bodies gave off. It was a bitter and unpleasant smell; not the salty smell of natural sex.

But the garden was full of sweet-smelling flowers that would conceal the bitterness; and some of the strangest scents were those of blossoms that opened after dark. It was now almost two in the morning; and the smells that rose from the darkened garden were giddyingly strong.

She called Kreiger's name again. Then she seemed to see him; a dark presence moving through the bushes.

If it was indeed Kreiger, why didn't he answer her call? Perhaps it wasn't him.

Keeping her silence now, she crept down the stairs and went out into the garden.

There was a gentle, balmy breeze tonight: it made the bushes and trees churn. The garden was large, and its lay-out complex, but she'd been playing here since she was a child. She could have found her way down its narrow, labyrinthine paths and around its rose patches and secret groves with her eyes closed.

She went directly to the place where she thought she'd seen the man when she'd been up at the bedroom window. Despite the sweetness of honeysuckle and the night-blooming jasmine, her nostrils caught the scent of something else, somebody else, in the vicinity. There was a stink that was not the bitter smell of her own body, or that of Kreiger. This was something else. Something that made her think of disease, of corruption, of death.

She stood very still. Something moved through the bushes close by. She saw its form, silhouetted against the starless sky: a vast misshapen head, armoured shoulders, the chest of an ox. Whatever it was, it walked with a pro-nounced limp, dragging its left leg. The closer it came to her the stronger the smell of corruption became. This trespasser was the source; no doubt of that.

Then, from the darkness close by, the sound of her lover's voice:

"Lucidique! Get away from here! Quickly!"

There was something broken in his voice.

"What's happened to you?" she said, afraid of the answer.

Hearing her voice, the trespasser looked in her direc-tion. A hood of flesh slid slickly back from the upper half of its face, revealing its skeletal features. This was—like them—a monster. And yet it was not like them. Not Agonistes' handiwork, at least. Not the product of the unsung architect of Eden.

This trespasser was a charnel-house child if ever there was one. It was made of parcels of rotten flesh and nerve and bone, all nailed together and given foetid breath.

She retreated as it strode towards her. She knew how to kill; that was not in doubt. But the creature still made her afraid. It was a powerhouse; and indifferent, she guessed, to any pain she might be able to cause it.

"Go!" she heard Kreiger yelling to her.

Her eyes flittered in his direction, and by the light shed from the bedroom window she saw him, on the ground, blood pouring out of him.

"Christ!"

She started towards him, but the trespasser moved to intercept her, its vast hands eager to tear out her throat.

But she wasn't going to flee the garden; not with her lover lying there in the dirt, bleeding from a hundred places. Instead she turned and led the limping slaughterer away from Kreiger, dodging through the darkened garden, using her knowledge of its layout to double the distance between them.

Still it came after her, throwing its weight through the tangle of thorny bushes; emitting a guttural din as it did so, like the noise of some immense mechanism that imperfectly copied the sound of a tormented animal; a bull, perhaps, beneath the slaughterer's hammer. It was horrible to hear.

She had come to the place where she hoped to outwit her pursuer: a tree which she had climbed a thousand times as a child, and now climbed again, so quickly that by the time the trespasser came in sight of it she was already concealed in its verdant canopy.

Now, she thought, if the beast would only wander beneath the tree, she could perhaps kill it. Drop out of the branches and cut open its throat. Even if it was something that was made from mortuary slops, it drew breath; and if she could open its throat from ear to ear, it would be dead as any other slitted thing.

But about six feet from the tree the creature stopped, and sniffed the air, looking around suspiciously. Did it sense that there was a trap laid for it here? She couldn't believe it had the wit to be so cautious. And yet it had halted, hadn't it? And now it retreated from the tree, loosing a low, barely audible noise in its throat, limping off into the darkness.

She carefully parted the foliage, to see if she could discover what it was up to. There was some sound from the direction in which she'd come, and then an audible moan from Kreiger.

Oh God, no, she thought. Don't let the trespasser be smart enough to use Kreiger as bait...

Her fears were realized a moment later, as the creature reappeared between the thorn bushes, dragging a heavy burden behind him. It was Kreiger, of course. This lover of hers, who was now reduced to little more than a sack, hauled behind the nameless fiend, had been a terror in his own right not so long ago. As the assassin Zarles Kreiger he'd once haunted the city of

Primordium from the shanties to the chateaus. Then, after the transformation worked upon him by Agonistes, as The Scythe-Meister, he'd wiped out the ruling class of the city in one scarlet night.

But now look at him! His face was torn open, as though the fiend had simply put his fingers into Kreiger's mouth (whose lips Lucidique had kissed an hour before) and ripped it apart like a paper bag. The rest of his body had been just as cruelly treated; the flesh torn away from its seating, exposing the breast-bone and the ribs and the long bone of his thigh. The loss of blood from these wounds was traumatic. It was a wonder Kreiger was still alive. But plainly—having been surprised in the garden while peacefully flower-picking—he'd fought back until he had no strength to fight with, at which point his attacker had sim-ply waited in the garden while one of its two victims slowly bled to death, knowing the other would appear given time.

And so she had. No doubt the creature had expected to dispatch her in a heartbeat; now it was obliged to coax her out of her hiding place with this bloody hos-tage. It grabbed Kreiger's neck and lifted him up by one hand, thrusting his broken face towards the tree. Kreiger's head lolled on his neck; his eyes rolled back into their sockets. He was as close to dead as made no difference.

Then his killer lifted its other hand and beckoned to the woman in the tree. As it did so it twitched Kreiger's head back and forth, like that of a doll. For Lucidique it was agonizing beyond words to see her lover, a man who had brought down a dynasty, bobbing around like a ventriloquist's doll. It made her lose all reason. Though she knew the trespasser below had the physical power to kill her, she could not watch Kreiger's last moments played out as a humiliating puppet-show.

She leapt from the tree with a shriek of rage, and before the creature could bring down its visor of flesh, she had slit both of its eyes with her weapon, blinding it.

It dropped Kreiger, and let out a roar that sounded pleasingly like panic. She ducked under its flailing arms and went to Kreiger.

He was dead.

She glanced back at his killer, who was indeed in a state of child-like terror. His roar had turned into howls that were close to descending into whimpers.

She could have wounded it again easily enough; and perhaps, after a dozen woundings, or two dozen, she might have claimed its life. But she didn't have any time to waste with the blinded thing. She needed to take Kreiger somewhere he had a hope of resurrection.

Out into the desert. Out to find Agonistes.

She lifted her lover's body up over her shoulders (he was lighter than she'd expected; troublingly so, as though the mass of his life had gone from him and would never be returned, even by a miracle). She would not let such pessimism linger in her mind, however. Leaving the blind trespasser to rage amongst the roses, she headed to the forecourt of the house. She gently laid the corpse in the back of the car, and then drove out of the city, in search of a sandstorm.

III

TALISAC LOOKED DOWN at the creature that had spilled from his body: his Mongroid. He'd seen prettier things, but then he'd seen uglier too. It had more self-reliance than any creature five minutes old should reasonably have; it walked, crab-like, on four hands; it made rudimentary attempts to express itself.

He called it to him, as he might a dog, but it wouldn't come. It was too interested in the bodies that lay everywhere about the chamber, examining them with its inverted head, sniffing at the ranker examples. It seemed to have a well-formed head, as far as Talisac could make out. There was some family resemblance there, he thought.

He had given up trying to draw its attention, but now—paradoxically—its eyes came to rest on him, and with its ungainly, sideways gait it approached him. It cast a glance around the charnel house as it did so, and its thought processes were perfectly clear. It was making the first distinction of its young life: between the living and the dead.

"That's right…" Talisac said, attempting an encouraging tone, "…they're dead. They're no use to you. I'm the one you have to help. I'm your father."

How much of this—if any—the Mongroid understood, Talisac had no idea. Very little, he guessed. But they had to begin somewhere. It would be a long, weary business, rearing this thing. He had hoped to give birth to something more praiseworthy; something he could show Montefalco, and thus be funded for further, more ambitious researches.

Now, he would have to do some fast-talking to get the General to see his vision of things. The crab homunculus produced from his sac of semen and sea-water was very far from the perfect, vicious child he'd hoped to produce: a hymn to the glories of testosterone.

But never mind, there would be others. In time he'd subdue this one, and vivisect it to see if he could work out where the errors lay. Then he'd try again.

The creature had come to a halt a few yards away from him, and was studying the sac in which it had been contained for seventeen weeks. Blood still dripped from it, onto the dirt floor. It scuttled over and put its tongue to the pool, tasting the fluid.

"No," Talisac said, faintly revolted by its display. "Don't do that."

He didn't want it getting some unnatural appetite; for blood, or flesh, or whatever other juices ran from him freely as he hung there. He was altogether too vulnerable in his present state.

"Bad," he said, effecting a tone of disgust. "Bad."

But the creature wasn't interested in being forbidden anything. It was a creature of instinct, and its instinct told it that there was a meal to be had here. It traced the source of the pool to the hanging corpse of flesh that had been its makeshift womb.

He didn't like the look in the creature's eyes at all. Nor did he like the way its belly was distending, as though its aroused appetite was awaking a change in its anatomy.

The Mongroid was pulling on the loose bloody tatters of his flesh now, its belly skin still swelling obscenely.

"Camille!" Talisac yelled, forgetting in his fear that the dwarf had left in the company of General Montefalco. He was alone.

And now, as he swung there, helpless, the belly of his offspring split open, revealing a vast mouth, completely arrayed with glistening teeth.

"Jesus! Oh Jesus!"

They were the last words Talisac uttered.

Using its four hands to spring up towards the womb from which he had so recently been delivered, the thing closed its gaping jaws on the groin of its parent, its teeth digging deep into Talisac's flesh. The cries to Jesus became a solid shriek. The Mongroid took a healthy mouthful of gut and manhood and womb, and dropped down to the ground again to devour what it had bitten off.

Talisac's innards, with their lower half removed, simply fell out of his body: uncoiling innards followed by liver and kidneys and spleen.

The genius of the Hospice of the Sacred Heart stopped screaming.

IV

THUS IN ONE night Primordium lost two of the monsters that had haunted its streets, and gained two new ones.

Venal Anatomica—or The Blind One, as he became known—was, in truth, something of a joke. Despite his bulk, and his phenomenal strength, he never developed the compensating skills that often come after a blinding.

He lived always as though he had just been blinded. Always flailing, always raging, always violent.

Montefalco took care of him, however, out of a bizarre sense of loyalty. He ordered that anyone found taunting the once mighty Venal Anatomica be summarily shot. After a dozen such casual executions, the message made it out to those who liked to torment the creature. The Blind One was left alone to haunt the city's graveyards, often digging up and eating the recently dead.

V

LUCIDIQUE NEVER FOUND Agonistes. Though she drove for several days, looking for the sandstorms where he hid himself, the desert was preternaturally still. Not a breeze to move so much as a grain of sand; much less a storm.

After a week, when The Scythe-Meister's body was beginning to smell, she dug a hole with her bare hands, and put him in it. Even as she sat there beside the mound, keening, she thought she heard Agonistes calling her name, and got up, ready at a moment's notice to reclaim Kreiger from his dry bed, and let the genius of Eden work his Lazarene magic on her lover.

But it was not the Resurrection she had heard. It was just a trick of the wind. Indeed, not once in the next forty-one years, during which time Lucidique seldom strayed more than a quarter of a mile from the place where Zarles Kreiger was laid, did Agonistes appear.

VI

THEN ONE DAY, waking to the same bright sky she'd woken to for over four decades—she was seized by a desire to see Primordium.

The house her father had built was still standing, she was surprised to find; left by authorities too superstitious to knock it down. She occupied it again, and after a few nights of sleeping on the bare boards overcame her fear of memories that would unknit her sanity, and moved up into the stained, ancient bed where she and Kreiger had made love all those years before.

There were no nightmares. He was with her, here, more than he'd ever been in the desert. He held her, in her dreams, and he whispered mischiefs to her, that sometimes she acted upon, for old time's sake. Blood she let freely, when it pleased her to do so. Nobody was safe from her. She would have happily murdered a saint if he'd looked at her in some fashion that irritated her.

And one night, just for the hell of it, she killed the three Generals, Montefalco, Bogoto and Urbano, who were by now fat and old and put up little protest at her arrival.

Another night, she went to find Kreiger's killer, The Blind One.

She found him in the cemetery, weeping from his slit eyes, the weary tears of a man who weeps every night, but knows no cure for them. She watched him for a while, while he wept and ate the dead. Then she left him to his suffering.

It was cruel, of course, to let him live, when she could have put him out of his misery with a well-placed blow. But why should she dispense mercy, when no one had ever been merciful to her? Besides, it pleased her to know that there were three monsters in Primordium. The Mongroid (whom she'd also gone to view in his excremental kingdom) in the sewers, Venal Anatomica in the charnel houses, she in her father's mansion. It had a certain neatness.

Sometimes, when she became lonely, she thought about going out into the desert, and lying down beside Kreiger's mummified corpse; letting the sand smother her. But something stopped her from doing it. Perhaps she'd have to watch the city of Primordium burn down first; or feel insanity creeping up her spine.

Until then, she would live out her destiny, in blood and tears and loneliness; in the knowledge that she was named in the prayers of tens of thousands of God-fearing citizens every night, who begged the Lord to keep them and their faces safe from her.

It was a land of immortality.